ISBN 978-1-0879-1159-5

First Printing, 2021

STORIES BY CHILDRE

FAMILY

STORIES BY CHILDREN
Volume 1

FAMILY
◇◇◇◇◇◇◇◇◇◇

FERNANCE AND CYRILLA FAMILY CLUB

FCFC

Contents

This book is dedicated to the children.

ACKNOWLEDGEMENTS

The Fernance and Cyrilla Family Club (FCFC) would like to acknowledge all those who, in any way, contributed to the completion and successful launch of this book. In particular our sponsors, the authors and their parents, the Board of Governors of the FCFC, and the Stories by Children Committee including, Chelsea Jno Baptiste, Valena Younis-Atilade, Carlyn Prince-Constant, Nicole Toussaint-Jno Baptiste, Hatty Leslie and Rosette Prince.

THE ADVENTURES OF THE PRINCE FAMILY

◇◇

By Dontae K. Carrington

Chapter One

Meet Fernance and Cyrilla Prince. They live on a tropical island paradise. They have superhero abilities. Fernance has super stretchy powers and Cyrilla can become invisible. Both of them can also fly. They spend most of their days in the garden and taking care of their 16 children. From now on we will refer to them as FP and CP. You need to remember this.

Yes, they had 16 children! One day the kids were playing outside. Suddenly, there was a loud bang and ka-poof! The first child lifted a boulder and threw it against a wall. When that happened FP and CP realized that all of their 16 kids would eventually become superheroes. No one knew about the superpowers of the Prince family. FP and CP would always talk to the children about keeping their superpowers hidden.

It was a Tuesday afternoon, and one of the children from the Prince family was playing with her friends at school. She looked up and saw an asteroid heading towards her island. She quickly gathered her siblings and went to the garden to find their parents. They told their parents what they had seen, and they came up with a plan to save the country.

The plan was to send two of their kids, Fedelia and Hatty, to destroy the asteroid. Hatty would freeze the asteroid to slow it down, and Fedelia would use her super strength to punch it into pieces. But the plan did not work. The asteroid was too big and fast for just the two of them. All of the Prince family came together to save the island from the asteroid. And they did...for now.

The asteroid stayed in orbit for 51 years before making its way back to Earth. But before I can tell you that story, I need to tell you another story.

Chapter Two

So the island was saved from the asteroid...for now, thanks to the Prince family. No actual records of pictures or videos of the event exist. I mean, it was the 1960's on a small island in the Caribbean. But the people in the community spoke about it for years. The story was passed down through generations.

Now, do you remember FP and CP? Well, they died. Yeah, I know it's sad, but they lived a good life. Their last days were spent in the garden that they loved so much. Fedelia eventually had kids of her own. Just 6 - she didn't have as many as CP and FP. She had a daughter named Dionne, and that's my mom. I can't reveal her age; she hates when I do that. Now Dionne had one child, just one. Her grandmother, CP, had 16, her mother, Fedelia, had 6 and she had 1. Do you see a pattern? 16..6..1...So that 1 child is me, Dontae.

My mom had super strength and speed, so I always assumed that I would have the typical superhero abilities like speed, strength or flight. My three cousins also had superhero powers. Jahrissa could fly, Kelano had super strength, and Phinix had speed. My superhero ability was intelligence. And it is a superpower! Because, **IF KNOWLEDGE IS POWER, THEN LEARNING MUST BE A SUPERPOWER!!!** I was always smart, like really smart. I could calculate and solve just about any problem. The abilities that my cousins and I had was a perfect combo! Intelligence, Strength, Speed, Flight.

Remember that asteroid from Chapter One? Well 51 years later it made its way back to Earth. That perfect combo that I spoke about...perfect for saving Earth from the asteroid. Now I will finally tell you how we saved Earth....in the next chapter. I promise it will be the final chapter, and I will make it short.

Chapter Three

So, it was left to Jahrissa, Kelano, Phinix and me, to save the Earth. The plan was simple; save Earth, save Dominica. First, we use INTELLIGENCE. Calculations tell me that the best way to destroy the asteroid was to wait until it enters the Earth's atmosphere. This time around, we want to destroy the asteroid, not just send it back into space. For this to work, I had to let the others know what to do and, most importantly, when.

Jahrissa used her power of FLIGHT to get Kelano further up into the atmosphere. Kelano used his super STRENGTH to break the asteroid up into small pieces. Finally, Phinix used his power of SPEED to collect the larger pieces and drop it into the ocean.

Believe it or not, the plan worked! It actually worked! I gave myself an **A++++++++** for the plan. I told you, INTELLEGENCE is a super power! And the carrying out of the plan by Jahrissa, Kelano and Phinix.....PERFECTO!!

The remaining asteroid fell as small pieces causing very little damage. We not only saved Dominica, but we saved over 7 BILLION people! Who knows what would have happened if the asteroid had crash landed on Earth?

After saving Earth, the entire world knew about us. There were so many pictures and videos being shared about the Prince family and how we saved the Earth. We became known as 'The Prince Family- Protectors of the Earth'. And that's our mission now - to Protect the Earth and its people. I know that FP and CP are no longer with us, but I think we are making them proud.

FAMILY CARES

By Joshua Saho

Family is Fun.

Family is Fair.

I love my Family,

Because they care.

A FOREVER FRIEND

By Sade Atilade

Family is a forever friend.

Family is always there for you.

Family is your love!

RIFAT

By Shoaib Ahmed

Rifat the cat, the fluffy orange cat,

The places you go are unknown.

But I do know the responsibility of taking care of you,

So if I don't care for you,

I can't call myself a cat owner.

I LOVE MY FAMILY

◇◇

By Humaira Ahmed

Roses are Red,

Violets are blue,

I love My Family

And everyone too!

PRINCESS ABBY

◇◇◇

By Abigail Saho

Chapter One

Once upon a time there was a pretty princess named Abby who lived in a beautiful castle. Every man in town wanted to marry her but no one could prove that they really loved her. One day the king had a gathering of the nearby princes. Their names were : James, Caleb, Aric, Shelly, Lawrence, and Trey. But the princess did not like any of them because James was very rude, Caleb was very inconsiderate, Aric was very unkind, Shelly was very selfish, Lawrence was very impolite and Trey was very heartless. So, the princess decided to set off on an adventure to find the love of her life.

A few days after the gathering, Abby packed her bag and she left the kingdom without anyone noticing. She headed off into the snowy mountains and went to another kingdom. She changed her name to Cindy, and she changed her clothes so no one would know that she was a princess.

The library was her favorite place in the new castle. One day she went into the library and an old man greeted her. "What are you looking for today, Miss?" asked the old man. "May I have a book to read, please?" replied Abby.

The princess went to a café to read her book. On her way, she saw a handsome man but he was not a prince, so she would not be allowed to marry him. When the man saw Abby he shouted, "That's the princess from the other kingdom." The princess was furious because the man had revealed her identity.

From the café, she strolled to a river, lay down in the river, and thought of what she would do. "I'll never find the love of my life now!" Abby thought.

But then... how did she get to the river and how is she not sinking? Abby woke up! She realized that she was still sitting in the café. The river stroll was just a dream.

Now that everyone knew who she really was, she had to leave. So, Abby packed her stuff again and went through the desert to the next nearby kingdom. Later that night, there was a midnight ball and Abby put on her finest clothes and went to the ball. There she saw the most handsome man. She thought about it for a minute and walked over to the man. His name was Jacob. Abby and Jacob fell in love at first sight, and they decided to go on a date the following week.

Chapter Two

"This is going to be great!" Abby thought. To get ready, Abby put on a beautiful yellow dress and texted Jacob to ask where they were going that night. It turned out that they were going to an amazing restaurant with delicious food. Jacob was so excited. Abby hoped that she had finally found the love of her life. When they got to the restaurant, she said, "You are looking awfully handsome today, Jacob."

Jacob replied, "You are looking awfully beautiful today, too." After that, they both laughed. Then they noticed that they had something in common - giving compliments.

Later that week, they went on their second date. It was amazing! After four more dates, they finally decided to get married. So Abby went back to the kingdom to tell her dad the good news. Her dad was happy to hear the good news. They put posters everywhere that soon Abby and Jacob were going to get married. Everyone in town was happy, and they held parties and parades to celebrate.

It was time for Abby and Jacob to get married. Abby walked down the hall with a beautiful white dress. Finally, Abby made her big decision to marry Jacob or not to marry Jacob. After two complete minutes of thinking, she said yes! They kissed and lived happily ever after.

Two years after Abby and Jacob got married, James, Caleb, Aric, Shelly, Lawrence, and Trey were ready to get their revenge. " Bwa ha ha-ha-ha-ha-ha-ha-ha " they all said. Their plan was very evil. When Abby and Jacob went out for dinner on their second wedding anniversary, Shelly dressed up as the waiter and poisoned Jacob's food.

Jacob was rushed to the hospital, and Abby hired a detective to figure out who poisoned him. After a few weeks, the detective discovered that Shelly was the one who poisoned Jacob, and he was arrested and sent to prison.

Abby's family stepped in to help. They paid all of Jacob's hospital bills. Soon Jacob was good and healthy, all thanks to Abby's family. Family is very important because without them, who would take care of you when you are young? Who would you have to love you?

HAPPY BUNCH

<><><><><><><><><><><><><><><><><><><><><><><><><><><><><><><><><><><><><><>

By Zendaya Robinson

We are a happy bunch!

Mother, grandma, sister and grandpa…
Sometimes we sing, sometimes we talk.
Sometimes we play, sometimes we pray.
What would we do without each other?
On special days like Christmas,
We all dress the same.
We share delicious meals;
The pies, the baked chicken and of course,
The tasty fruit cake.
These bring joy and gladness to my family.

I love my family and would not trade it for any other!

F - Friends

A - Appreciation

M - Memories

I - Initiative

L - Love

Y - Yearning

MY MOM

By Imani Henry

It's a happy day.

My mother is here.

One hug from her and all dark clouds clear.

All in all, she's pretty fair.

She shows me much love.

She's more graceful than a dove.

Not just me, but my family agrees,

That my mom's beyond compare.

Something that puzzles me

Is how my mom carries

All her responsibilities,

And still has time for me.

Mother, I love you.

Everything I do.

It's all for you.

My dad and I admire you,

You know this is true.

FAMILY AND YOU

◇◇◇

By Hilkiah Constant

Family.

Without family,

There would not be a You.

You would not be able to live.

Family!

Family.

You could not be,

What you possibly could be,

Without a family that cares.

Family!

In a family,

You will be filled with joy.

And get the support to fulfill your destiny.

Family!

MY DAY AT THE RIVER WITH MY FAMILY

By Kelano Pascal

One Sunday, my family and I went to the river to enjoy the cool water and to look out for hermit crabs which my bigger cousin told me about. When we got there, the sun was peeking out from the clouds, so it was not too hot. The sunlight made the river look nice and shiny. I found a lot of things along the riverbank, which I called my treasures. The first thing I found was a pretty red rock, shaped oval like an egg, and then I found a lot of empty shells. But still no hermit crab!

My mom told me that if I am patient, before I leave, I may just be lucky to find at least one hermit crab. Just then my aunt pointed out a group of beautiful red and gold fish, swimming in the river. I also saw periwinkles (veeyo) on the rocks in the water. But still no hermit crab!

Soon it was time to bathe, and my baby cousin came into the water to bathe with me. My mommy and my friend, Roy, made little pools in the river using stones from the river bank. We made big splashes in the water and that was a lot of fun. I even tried to swim a bit.

We were almost ready to get out of the water, when Roy took me to the other side of the river. As soon as I reached across the river, I spotted a hermit crab. I touched it and right away it went to hide inside its shell. I collected 6 hermit crabs and placed them in my little beach bucket, where my little cousin, my aunt and mom enjoyed watching them move around trying to find a way out of the bucket.

Not too long after, my mom said it was time to leave. So, we packed up, got dressed, and sadly left the riverside before the sun went down. This, for me, was my favorite memory of being at the river with my family. Family means everything to me!

SAVED BY A BEANSTALK

By Keyondre Prevost

I am Jack. The giant claims that I am a terrible person but, really, I am not! Now listen to my version of what really happened.

My mom did not give me any snacks to eat when she sent me to my bedroom that night. I looked out the window and saw a big bean stalk. My dad had only planted the beans yesterday after my mom got it from the supermarket. I was surprised that it got big so fast! I opened the window and climbed up the beanstalk. It was very tall.

When I reached the top, I was next to a house, so I jumped down and lightly knocked on the front door. A lovely lady opened the door and I asked for some food. She told me to come inside. She gave me a jam sandwich and some apple juice. I took one bite and then I heard and felt the floor rumbling! The lady quickly hid me in the oven. From the oven, I could see a giant in the room. He was huge! He looked really scary and mad. He was shouting at the lady.

I saw a cupboard and thought it might have food. I slowly sneaked out of the oven and crawled to the cupboard. I opened the door and there was no food, only shiny gold pieces. I took some and put them in my pocket. A gold piece suddenly dropped with a big clink sound! The giant turned around and saw me. I started running out of the kitchen and down the hallway. The giant was chasing me. I made it to the front door and luckily it was open! I ran out to the bean stalk and started climbing down quickly. I could see the giant, but he wasn't as fast as me.

I got down and asked my mum for an axe. She started helping me to cut down the tree. My dad heard the noise and came to see what it was about. When he saw, he went in and got a chainsaw. We cut down the beanstalk quickly because we worked together as a family. The giant came tumbling down and hurt himself.

I only took a few pieces of gold, because he had a lot. He was mean and did not share. I wanted to give it to my mum because she likes shiny things.

FAMILY IS SPECIAL

By Glendora Etienne

My family is a special one. It consists of my mom, sister, granny and me. My grandpa, who is not living with us, is always around and when he comes home, he greets my sister and I with these words, "Girls them!" My grandpa is a loving man.

We live in the most beautiful community of Grand Fond, in the South East of Dominica. My family grows dasheen, cassava, cocoa and vegetables. Though not grown on a large scale, we share with our relatives and friends and the rest brings in a little income.

Growing up in this family is fun. My mom and granny cook interesting and delicious meals. Whenever I hear of dishes like fig pie and baked chicken, I am ready to eat a lot. I love to do chores around our home, like sweeping and mopping, and washing plates and clothes. I just love my family!

ON THE NUMBER 6

By Sajjad Ahmed

Me and my brothers play from day until night. They crowd any
sorrows with bliss and delight.

Our sister, although innocent, makes sure to pressure me as a
figure, like a governor to a province.

My father, with the voice of a lion, would vouch enormously
for each of the children under his shelter.

And my mother, despite physical aches from tension, still
carries our problems on her boat of cultivation.

The people who care, shield, and embrace me are my family.
A family of six.

FOR LOVE

By Hadassah Constant

Family, a body of love and strength.

Family means helping each other and being there.

Family means you are a part of something very wonderful.

Family! This and happiness are the two most important things
in life.

Family is home not a place.

Family, their love is like no other.

Family isn't only bound by blood or last names but by
dedication and love.

Family is having each other's back and choosing to love
even on our worst days.

THE BOND OF FAMILY

By Giana and Gabrielle Oscar

1.

Family is made of happiness and sadness - LOVE and tears.
The bond grows closer as the years go by.

2.

More precious with the making of unforgettable memories.
Family is made up of ones you dislike only for a while - but
your LOVE is eternal.

3.

It's a precious gift whose value is not found in numbers but in
its capacity to LOVE.
It's the place where you find someone to push you on and
believe in you - Celebrate with you and comfort you in times
of need.

4.

Family is where your heart feels in place because you are always
needed,

always welcomed,
always wanted,
always LOVED.

LOVE + COMMUNITY + HELP = FAMILY

By Abigail Saho

What does family mean to me?

Intro

My name is Abigail and I am connected to the Prince Dynasty family through the Younis family. I am 8 years old and in second grade at Lockheed Elementary School. I live with my mom and brother, and sometimes with my dad.

Love

I love all my family members. I learned about love from being with family. For example, one time when I went to my aunty Valena's house and met my cousins I felt very loved because they accepted me for who I am. Also, I discovered we like the same things. I was so happy!

Community

My family is always making fun zooms. For example, one time we had a secret Santa zoom and everyone got real presents. This is an example of how we come together as a community. It was so much fun!

Help

Sometimes, for the zoom topics, they share health information. Sharing zoom topics about health is helpful because, as family members, we might have the same health issues. I think the Prince Dynasty group tries their best to make sure that everyone is safe and healthy.

F.A.M.I.L.Y

By Abigail Saho

WHAT FAMILY MEANS TO ME

By Christopher Atilade

The Fernance and Cyrilla Family Club (FCFC) is an organization formed by descendants of Fernance and Cyrilla Prince of Grand Fond, Dominica. Since its inception in January 2018, the Club has engaged in a number of social, educational, and charitable activities. In January 2021, the FCFC embarked on the Stories by Children literary movement which aims to create excitement about reading and writing, and provide an avenue for creative expression, while boosting the self-esteem of the children.

ABOUT THE AUTHORS

Abigail Saho, affectionately known as Abby, is an energetic and creative 9-year-old who resides in Marietta, Georgia. Her hobbies include cooking, coloring, dancing, drawing, and gaming. She also enjoys reading. Some of her favorite books are from the Baby-Sitters Club Collection by Ann M. Martin and Raina Telgemeier. At school, her favorite subjects are math and writing. Although Abby has her eyes set on working to fight crime, she has not quite decided on a specific career path. In the future, she hopes to be an entrepreneur and create jobs for herself and others. Her favorite color is purple because it stands for royalty.

Christopher Atilade, affectionately called Chris by family and friends, is an eleven-year-old rising 6th grader. At school, his favorite subject is math simply because it is easy! In his spare time, Chris likes playing computer games and listening to music. He enjoys all music genres; however, his favorite is pop. His all-time favorite computer game is Roblox. Some of Chris' favorite things to do include watching TV with family and going to the beach especially in Dominica! Chris loves pizza and his mom's pasta dishes. His favorite books to read are from the Diary of a Wimpy Kid book series by Jeff Kinney. As it relates to the future and career, Chris has not thought about it yet but plans to let life carry him through. Chris loves all shades of blue.

Dontae K. Carrington, is a 7-year-old who wishes to live in a world where kindness is the rule rather than the exception. 'The Adventures of Captain Underpants' is his all-time favorite book series. His favorite quote is, " If knowledge is power then learning is a super power." At school, he enjoys mathematics and science. Dontae likes to keep busy after school with ninja warrior training, martial arts, swimming, gaming and working with his father. He is unsure of what he wants to be when he grows up, but he is convinced that whatever he chooses, he will succeed.

Folasade Atilade, or Sade as she prefers to be called, is a warm-spirited 9-year-old who is looking forward to 3rd grade this fall. At school, Sade enjoys math because it is fun, and she gets to learn new things. In her spare time, she enjoys playing Roblox and Mancala. She also enjoys playing with chalk and slime. For Sade, slime is all about the sounds, stretchability, and textures. "Slime is fun, and you can make so many different shapes." Some of Sade's favorite things include going to the pool, popsicles, and mac and cheese from Outback. Her favorite toy is Rainbow High Dolls, and her favorite TV shows include Night Fox, I am Sana, and Oblivious HD. In the future Sade hopes to be a Nail Technician and open her own Nail Salon. She is intrigued by the creativity and art involved in it. Sade's favorite color is purple.

Gabrielle Emaline Jael Oscar, is an 8-year-old student of the St. Martin Primary School. She was born on April 15th 2013. Her favorite color is pink. One of her favorite books is from the Junie B Jones collection titled, 'Junie B Jones and Her Big Fat Mouth'. Her favorite subject at school is mathematics. In her spare time, she enjoys reading but most of all she enjoys playing. In her very own words, "Mammy, when I grow up, I want to be an accountant".

Imani Henry, is a bright and articulate 11-year-old who resides in Checkhall, Dominica, and attends the Pioneer Prep School. Imani's favorite subject in school is Social Studies because "There is a lot of history behind it, and you understand better when you have fun and imagine while you learn." He loves books! His favorite book series is the Diary of a Wimpy Kid collection by Jeff Kinney. He describes himself as a very creative and imaginative person. He remembers making 'little cards' for his parents when he was younger, just because. Imani also enjoys playing video games. Imani's favorite color is orange. He describes orange as not being only one color; it has shades which are so colorful and, according to him, "You just feel like it's a joyful color honestly." Most of all, Imani loves his pets a lot; he has a dog named Blade and a goat named Sharpie.

Glendora Rohanna ZiWei Ettienne, an energetic 7-year-old who attends the Grand Fond Primary School, was born on the 21st day of February 2014. Glendora loves the colour purple. Her favorite subject is science. In her spare time, she enjoys reading and playing teacher game with her friends. When she has no friends around to play with, she reads to her teddies. Glendora wants to be a teacher, when she grows up.

Hadassah Jada Constant, is a beautiful, creative and energetic 14-year-old. She is fondly called Dassy. She was born on July 8th 2006, on the island of Dominica. Her favorite pass times are reading, singing, listening to music, and doing ballet. From an early age, she always said she wants to become a doctor. Dassy's favorite color is purple, and the food she enjoys the most is lasagna. There's never a dull moment with her around. Everyone needs a Dassy in their life.

Humaira Ahmed, is a 5-year-old who loves a world where animals and humans live happily together. With 'The Princess and The Pea' being her favourite story, Humaira expresses her love for beautiful and magical things through her drawings and artwork almost every day. At school, she enjoys mathematics and writing. After school, Humaira loves to design dresses, sew, and play video games with her three brothers. Humaira wants to be a veterinarian when she grows up and believes that God, family and love is more important than anything.

Giana J'nae Francis Oscar, is a 13-year-old 2nd form student of the Convent High School, in Dominica. She was born on the 27th of September 2007. Her favorite color is purple, and her hobbies are dancing and cooking. A book that she loves a lot is '13 Reasons Why'. At school her favorite subject is History. Currently, she is a club member of Dance, 4-H and Girl Up!. Her dream is to become a Pediatrician/Real Estate Agent and an Entrepreneur.

Joshua Saho, is a clever 7-year-old, affectionately called Josh or Joshie by family and friends. At school, Josh's favorite subject is math because it is fun and challenging. His favorite stories are from the Dogman book series by Dav Pilkey. Josh's hobbies include gaming, playing with beyblades, chess, soccer, and sprinting. He also enjoys watching TV and solving riddles. His favorite TV shows include PJ Masks and Wolfoo. When he grows up, Josh hopes to solve crimes as a Police Officer and wants to be a businessman. His favorite color is yellow because it is the color of the sun.

Kelano Andre Azriel Pascal, was born on the 21st of October 2016 in Dominica. His favorite colour is red, and his hobbies are singing, playing football, acting and picture reading. When he grows older, he wants to be a doctor and a fire officer. He has two favorite stories; they are 'The Ninjabread Man' by C. J. Leigh, and 'The Berenstain Bears, That's So Rude!' by Mike Berenstain. In his spare time, he loves to be read to, and he likes watching animated movies.

Sajjad Ahmed, is a 15-year-old boy who loves computers, video games and trading card games. He frequently runs tournaments with his younger siblings. At school, his favorite subjects are IT and history. Sajjad aspires to be a computer programmer when he gets older. Sajjad loves animals and spends a lot of time chilling with his mini tiger, Rifat. He loves spending his free time going to the beach and diving.

Keyondrè Jeremiah Prevost, is 6 years old. He was born on October 7th 2014. Keyondre enjoys playing outside with friends and playing Roblox. He likes the color yellow best. His favourite story is 'The Singing Chef'. Keyondre' wants to be a builder when he grows up. He wants to build apartments.

Shoaib Ahmed, is a 9-year-old boy who enjoys playing video games with his older brothers and little sister. At school, his favorite subjects are social sciences and mathematics. Shoaib loves to play with his peers. He also enjoys experimenting with making robots out of household items. When he grows up, he wants to be a robotics engineer. Shoaib loves gardening, discovering new plant species, and learning everything he can about plants and the world around him.

Zendaya Yohanna ZhenAi Robinson, is an 8-year-old student of Grand Fond Primary School. She was born on the 26th day of November 2012. Her favorite colour is Pink. In her spare time she enjoys reading, watching animated movies, and playing dominos with her grandmother. Her favorite subject is Language Arts. Zendaya says she would like to be a teacher when she gets older just like her Aunt Hatty.

Hilkiah Constant, is a 13-year-old fourth former who loves music, gaming and cooking. His favorite subjects are French and Computer Science. He hopes to be a Computer Engineer in the future. Music being his first passion, he plays the trombone, trumpet, drums, tuba as well as some guitar, bass and keyboards. He also hopes to be a chef – even if it's only for his family. His kind and considerate heart makes him a pleasure to know and be around.

Download Your Free Activities Book!

Visit our website, www.storiesbychildren.org
to download your free activities and colouring
book which includes all the illustrations of
Stories By Children Volume 1 - Family.

Thank You!

Want to be published in Stories by Children?

ANNOUNCING STORIES BY CHILDREN, VOLUME 2

When I Grow Up!

◇◇◇

Following a successfull launch of Stories by Children, Volume 1 - Family, the FCFC is proud to announce the theme of Stories by Children, Volume 2 - **When I Grow Up!**

All children of Dominica and the diaspora, under the age of 16, are invited to submit a piece of writing, such as a short story, poem or prose, to The Stories by Children Literary Competition. Up to TEN winning entries will be selected and published in Stories by Children, Volume 2 in **Fall of 2022**.

All submissions must be in by **11:59 PM, on Febuary 28th, 2022.** The winners will be announced on **March 31st, 2022**. The submission link can be found on FCFC Stories by Children Instagram and Facebook pages as well as on the website - www.storiesbychildren.org.

Follow "FCFC Stories by Children" on Facebook and Instagram to stay up to date with competiton announcements and other FCFC Stories by Children News! More information on the Stories by Children Literary Competition can be found on www.storiesbychildren.org.

◇◇◇

FERNANCE AND CYRILLA FAMILY CLUB